The Berenstain Bears
GET THEIR KICKS

All soccer moms know
it's a new game, Bub,
when a big ol' papa bear
can learn from his cub.

A First Time Book®

The Berenstain Bears
GET THEIR KICKS

Stan & Jan Berenstain

Random House 🏠 New York

Library of Congress Catalog Number: 97-076109   ISBN 0-679-88955-8 (trade) — 0-679-98955-2(lib. bdg.)
Printed in the United States of America   10 9 8 7 6 5 4 3 2 1

Papa Bear's family, friends, and neighbors all knew that he was a "traditional" sort of fellow. That means he liked to do the things he'd always done in pretty much the same ways he'd always done them. He liked to use traditional tools in his work as a woodsbear— though he did use more modern tools when he absolutely had to.

He was a shirt-and-overalls kind of guy when it came to clothes. He was a meat-and-potatoes kind of guy when it came to food. And when it came to sports, Papa was devoted to the games he'd grown up with: football in the fall, basketball in the winter, and in the summer, baseball, of course.

Papa loved baseball:

the smack of the ball
in the catcher's mitt,

the pull on the shoulders
after that first hard swing,

THWOCK

the loud *"thwock!"* of the ball on the bat when you hit a high fly over the fielder's head.

So when cubs Brother and Sister fell head over heels in love with soccer, Papa Bear got a little upset—especially when it turned out that Mama, who had played soccer as a cub, had signed up as coach for the neighborhood league.

So it was that on a bright sunny summer day, Papa bounded out of the tree house with a bat, a ball, and three gloves: a catcher's mitt for himself and two fielder's gloves for Brother and Sister.

"Get ready for some baseball!" he shouted.

"We'll shag some flies, work on the curve, and field some grounders!"

"Er, maybe some other time, Papa," said Brother. "But we're going to be busy today."

"Busy doing what?" asked Papa.

"Playing soccer," said Brother.

"Soccer?" said Papa. "You mean that game they play with that funny black-and-white ball?" Papa could hardly believe his ears. "Do you mean you'd rather play soccer than *baseball*?"

"Maybe we can play baseball later this afternoon," said Brother. "But soccer tryouts are today, and we have to get over to the soccer field for some early practice."

"That's right," said Sister. "I'm going to try out for the Kewpies."

"That's the younger team," said Brother. "I'm going to try out for the Buddies."

"The Kewpies? The Buddies?" said Papa. "What kind of team names are they? What's wrong with good old-fashioned baseball team names like Tigers, Sluggers, and Giants? Besides, I don't see why you have to practice. All you have to do is run around and kick that silly black-and-white ball once in a while."

"There's a lot more to soccer than that," said
Mama. She had just come out of the house. It said
"Soccer Mom" on her shirt.
"Like what?" asked Papa.
"Like all sorts of stuff," said Brother. "Like
dribbling, passing, trapping, and headers."
"And all different kinds of kicks," added Sister.

"*Humph!*" humphed Papa. "I've never played soccer in my life," he said. "But I'll bet I can kick that silly ball farther and straighter than all three of you put together. Here, gimme that ball!"

Papa put the ball on the ground, stepped back a long way, and said, "See those two birch trees way over there?" The two birch trees were quite far away.

Then Papa charged forward at full speed. But he misjudged his kick, missed the ball completely, and landed on the ground with a mighty *"Oof!"*

OOF!

Mama and the cubs ran to Papa.

"Are you all right, dear?" said Mama as she and the cubs helped Papa get up.

"Of course I'm all right," said Papa. "Just let me try that again."

"Sorry, my dear," said Mama, picking up the ball. "But we must be on our way. Come along, cubs."

Papa watched as "Soccer Mom" Mama and the cubs headed for the soccer field, dribbling and passing as they went.

"Farther and straighter than all three of them put together," said Papa as he stared at a large stone that lay on the ground. "I'll show 'em!" he snarled, and he kicked the stone with all his might.

But it wasn't a stone at all. It was the top of a big buried rock.

"Y-E-E-E-O-W-W-W!" cried Papa as he hopped around holding his foot.

Y-E-E-O-W-W-W!

As Papa sat on a low stump rubbing his foot, he heard sounds coming from the soccer field, which lay just over the hill. "Maybe there's more to soccer than I thought," he said. "I think I'll go have a look." He limped off in the direction of the noise.

When Papa arrived at the field, he saw that there was, indeed, more to soccer than he'd thought—a lot more! There were cubs and coaches all over the field practicing. There were league officials moving among them, writing things down on clipboards.

Brother and Sister were right at the center of the action, learning different moves along with all the other cubs. They were learning:

SLOW IT DOWN EASY.

KEEP IT CLOSE TO YOUR FEET.

the trap,

the dribble,

KEEP YOUR EYE ON THE BALL.

the pass,

the instep kick,

the volley,

and, of course, the header.

And who was teaching the header but "Soccer Mom" Mama herself.

And what's more, they had to do all those things without touching the ball with their hands! Baseball-loving Papa couldn't help being impressed.

The cubs and Mama were so busy with their dribbles, kicks, and headers that they didn't see Papa. But Papa saw them, and he was rooting hard for his cubs to make their teams.

He also saw the league officials hand their reports to a bear who was wearing a sweatshirt that said "Commissioner."

Papa sidled over to the commissioner, who was studying the reports. "Er, sir," said Papa. "Have Sister and Brother Bear made their teams? I'm their dad."

"As a matter of fact, they have," said the commissioner. "Sister made the Kewpies and Brother made the Buddies. Now, if you'll excuse me, I'm just about to post the results."

"How about that!" said Papa with a big grin. He felt so good that he forgot all about his sore foot as he hurried home.

"Say," said Brother as they headed over to see the tryout results. "Isn't that Papa?"

"Hmm," thought Brother and Sister and Mama as they watched Papa head for home.

Brother and Sister were very happy to have made their teams. But they hadn't forgotten their promise to play a little baseball with Papa. They got the ball, bat, and gloves.

"How about a little baseball, Papa?" said Brother. "Here, catch!" he cried as he tossed the ball to Papa. But Papa didn't catch it. He gave it a header instead.

It was a good thing he was wearing his soft brown hat or he might have gotten himself a big headache. As it was, it knocked him down.

The cubs and Mama ran over to him. "Papa! Papa!" cried Brother. "Why did you do that?"

"Oh, I just wanted to show you that if soccer is good enough for my cubs, it's good enough for me. I'll tell you what. Instead of playing a little baseball, why don't you two show me some of your best soccer moves?"

And Brother and Sister did—
while "Soccer Mom" Mama
and "Soccer Dad" Papa
watched proudly.